FAME MOUSE

Written by Joshua George

Illustrated by Barbara Bakos

Licensed exclusively to Top That Publishing Ltd
Tide Mill Way, Woodbridge, Suffolk, IP12 1AP, UK
www.topthatpublishing.com
Copyright © 2015 Tide Mill Media
All rights reserved
2 4 6 8 9 7 5 3 1
Manufactured in China

ISBN 978-1-78445-429-6

A catalogue record for this book is available from the British Library

For Oak, the most famous boy in Easton.

In an ordinary mouse-hole house,
Lived an extra-ordinary mouse;
A mouse of such stupendous fame
That **Fame-Mouse** was his name!

STAR
certification

Fame
mouse

Animals came from near and far,

some came by train,

some came by car,

some came by plane,

some came by bus,

Meerkat Express

the meerkats made an awful fuss!

There was a sign outside the door ...

A line stretched round outside the house,
All waiting to see **Fame-Mouse!**

A platypus, porcupine and three seals,
Seven piglets filled the air with squeals!
Two lions lined up behind a cow,

(the ants were all jumbled anyhow).

A toucan said to a kangaroo,
'I can't wait to see him, how about you?'

The kangaroo bounced, and hopped, and leapt,
`I'm so excited, I've hardly slept!'

Right at the front pushed a herd of sheep,
Piled one on the other, a big woolly heap!
The crowd grew **noisier** outside the house,
All waiting to see **Fame-Mouse!**

FAME MOUSE

STAR TODAY!

HERE!
from 9 till 4

Then a crow flew by and said, `Ca-caw! What's that mouse so famous for?´

'I mean does he dance or anything,
Or is he some sort of mousey king?'

FAME
MOUSE

The crowd fell silent ... no one was sure ...
What **was** Fame-Mouse so famous for?

Perhaps he could act? Or maybe sing?
Crow laughed, `He can't do anything!´

At that the animals began to boo,
Snakes and otters and emu too!

The smallest meerkat jumped up and spoke,

'Famous for nothing? What a joke!'

A bear wandered off in a dreadful grump,
A camel grunted, `I've got the hump!'
All of them left in a cloud of dust,

The elephants trumpeting in disgust.

But Cat licked his lips thoughtfully,
`I think that I might stay for tea.´